Ms Blakely

Danny

Parker

Zoe

Mario

Emma

Jonah

Leo

Alexis

Jakey

Danny

Parker

Aubrey

Maddy

Bruce

Danny

Dear Reader,

This book is special! The guide below will help you understand the symbols.

 = Turn to the next page.

 = Turn to the page that your choice says to go to, and continue reading from there.

⬑ = This shows you which page you came from, so ONLY use it if you want to go back and change your last choice.

End #1 = You've reached one of the eight different endings! To reach another ending, start at the beginning and make different choices. Try to reach all 8!

—

What Should DANNY DO?
School Day

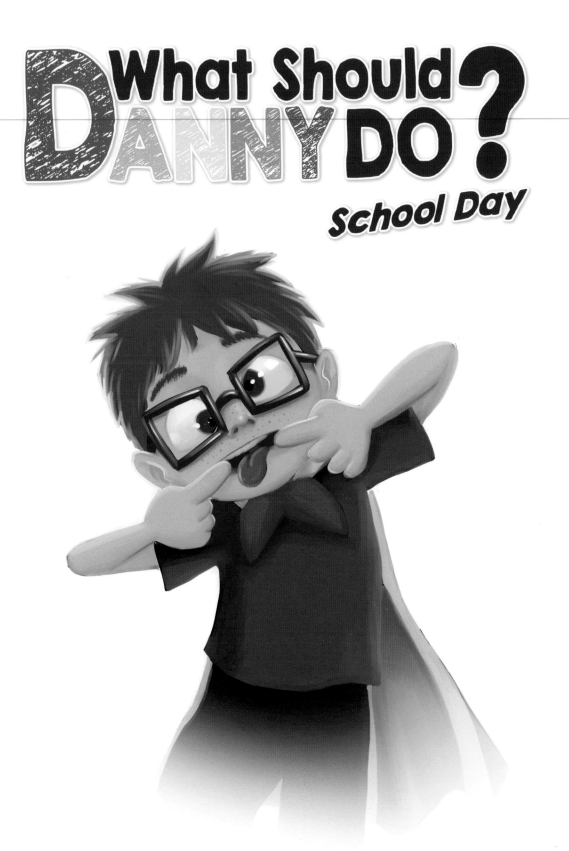

Ganit & Adir Levy
Illustrated by Mat Sadler

Hi! My name is Danny, and I'm a superhero in training.
I have lots of cool superpowers.

I can make myself invisible.

I'm super strong.

I have x-ray vision.

And even though learning how to fly is harder than I thought it would be... I'm not giving up anytime soon.

I've been testing a superpower called the POWER TO CHOOSE at home, and today I'm going to practice using it at school. With this power, I can change my day by changing my choices.

Today is a special day because you'll be making choices for me! When you reach an ending, you can start over and change your choices. Then we'll see how powerful the POWER TO CHOOSE really is.

Ready? Let's go!

Oh, no! This morning I was caught by the evil Dr. Ninjario! But have no fear. After a hundred thousand minutes, I'm finally on the brink of escaping. His laser beam dungeon is no match for me!

"Danny, it's time to get ready for school!" Mommy calls out.

Aw, man! I'm busy trying to escape from Dr. Ninjario! If I stop now

What Should DANNY Do?

Continue playing? Go to page 20
Stop playing and get ready for school? Go to page 36

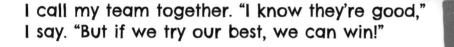

I call my team together. "I know they're good,"
I say. "But if we try our best, we can win!"

We start playing, and the game is super close.
With less than a minute left we're down by four
points. I get the ball and use my super speed
to run to the hoop. I jump super high and
score! Yes! Now we're down by just two points.

Jonah takes the ball out, but Alexis steals it! She
passes the ball to me. "Hurry, Danny!" she yells.
"There isn't much time left."

I dribble straight to the three-point line and throw the ball up towards the basket. If I make this shot, we'll win the game!

The bell rings as the ball flies through the air. Everyone watches and holds their breath. The ball rolls around the rim, but flies out. Aw, man! So close!

Jonah breathes a sigh of relief as we walk to class. "You played great, Danny," he says. "I didn't think your team had a chance, but you almost won at the buzzer."

"Thanks," I say.

I'm happy I decided to play instead of give up.

In class, Ms. Blakely is teaching us how to use a number line in math. I don't like standing in line to go to recess, so I don't understand why numbers need to stand in line either! This is confusing.

"Does anyone have any questions?" she asks.

I look around, and it seems like everyone else understands. If I raise my hand, my friends might laugh at me. I'm not a clown, I'm a superhero!

What Should DANNY Do?

Raise his hand to ask a question? Go to page 28
Not raise his hand? Go to page 46

I'm a little scared of Parker, but then I remember I'm a superhero. If I don't stop him, who will?

I think I need a sidekick for this mission.

"Hey, Jakey. Let's go tell him to stop," I say.

"OK, as long as we go together."

I summon my super bravery and walk up to Parker. "If you aren't nice to us, we won't play with you!" I say.

"Yeah!" Jakey says.

Then, Maddy, Micah and Josh say that they won't play with him either if he isn't nice.

Parker is surprised. "I don't care," he says. "Don't play."

We all go over to the next field to start a new game. Just before we start, Maddy gives me a hug. "Thanks for standing up for me, Danny!"

But then I see Parker all alone. I know I'd feel sad if I didn't have anyone to play with. Maybe Parker just needs a friend.

I run over to him. "Hey, Parker. We want you to play," I say. "We just want you to play nicely with everyone."

"I don't want to play," he says.

"Well, you're one of the best players. We want you back," I say.

"I'm not in the mood," Parker says.

"Here, this might help," I say. "You can wear it for the rest of recess."

We run back to the field. Parker's really nice for the rest of the game. I wonder if it's my cape that did the trick.

Later, my super muscles beg to be recharged. Luckily, it's lunch time.

I see Leo sitting all by himself. He looks sad. If I stop to ask him what's wrong, it might take too long till I get to eat. My super muscles won't like that!

What Should DANNY Do?

Pretend not to notice Leo's sad? Go to page 32

Ask Leo what's wrong? Go to page 40

There's no way I'll let Dr. Ninjario beat me! I find my way through the laser beams and finally reach the ladder to the secret escape hatch. Just then, Mommy calls out, "Three minutes till the bus is here!"

Three minutes? Aw, man. Dr. Ninjario had me tangled in a time warp!

I hurry to get dressed, but finding my other shoe takes forever.

Then, I remember that today is show-and-tell. I quickly grab Webster, my tarantula, and put him in my backpack.

I run outside, but I'm too late.

Daddy takes me to school, so he'll be late to work. He doesn't seem happy about that.

I finally get to school and zoom to class. I'm late, so I don't get to sit next to my best friends Maddy and Jakey during show-and-tell.

I tiptoe to an empty spot and wait for my turn. Finally, Ms. Blakely calls me up.

I reach into my backpack, but Webster isn't there. *Uh-oh!*

"I can't find Webster," I say.

"Is he a hamster?" Miss Blakely asks.

"No, he's a..."

Just then, Maddy shrieks. "AAAAAAAAAAAAAAH!"

I zoom to grab Webster, but Maddy is still mad.

"How could you let him loose!?!" Maddy asks.

"It was an accident!"

"I know it was an accident," Ms. Blakely says, "but you'll have to be more responsible. Please find a way to keep your tarantula safe and away from others."

I find what I need and build a cage, but by the time I'm done, I'm late to recess!

Aw, man. The soccer game already started, and that's my favorite sport. They're still picking teams for basketball, so I use my super speed to rush over there.

Alexis picks me, but the teams end up so unfair! Jonah, Sarah, Mario, and Paul are all so good.

I'm worried. Even with my superpowers, there's no way we can win!

What Should DANNY Do?

Leave and look for something else to play? Go to page 30
Try his best and have fun no matter what? Go to page 10

I know I can figure this out with a little help! I turn on my super focus and raise my hand. "How am I supposed to use the number line to get the answer?" I ask.

"That's a great question, Danny," Ms. Blakely says.

She explains it again, and I finally get it! Score!

I finish my worksheet and double-check it. Mario whispers to me, "Thanks for asking that question, Danny. I wasn't sure what I was doing."

When I get home, Mommy asks me how my day was. I tell her everything that happened.

"Sounds like your day was OK," she says. "Do you think that was because of how you used your POWER TO CHOOSE?"

"I think so," I say. "And if I use it even more wisely tomorrow, I might have an even better day."

End #5

I won't play with teams this unfair. I walk off the court.

"Come on, Danny," Alexis calls. "They'll have more players than us if you don't play."

"I don't care," I say. "We'll lose anyway."

27

I look for something else to play, but nothing looks fun. I'm super bored.

After recess Maddy seems upset.

"I thought your spider would kill me," she says.

I laugh. "Tarantulas can't kill you!"

"It's not funny, Danny! I don't want to play with you for the rest of the day." She stomps away.

Back in class, Ms. Blakely is teaching some new math. I'm not in the mood. I can't stop thinking about how mean Maddy was to me.

What Should DANNY Do?

Apologize to Maddy for letting Webster loose? Go to page 70
Find a way to get even with Maddy for being mean? Go to page 50

I use my super speed to zoom past Leo. I don't look back in case he's looking at me.

I sit down and take a few bites out of my sandwich, but then I notice that none of my friends came to sit with me.

I look around and see that they're sitting next to Leo, talking and having a good time. *Is Leo their new best friend?*

Later in class, it's time for science. I normally love science, but I'm still wondering why Maddy and Jakey left me for Leo.

On the bus ride home, I sit alone, and that's no fun.

But then, Maddy and Jakey come and sit next to me like nothing ever happened.

"Hey," I say. "So I guess Leo's your new best friend now."

"No way, Danny," Maddy says. "You'll always be our best friend. We just saw that Leo was really sad because he forgot his lunch at home. So we offered him some of our food."

"Oh," I say. Maybe if I would have used my POWER TO CHOOSE to ask Leo what was wrong, I would have been able to help him too. Looks like that would have made the rest of my day way better.

End
#3

I'm having so much fun, but I know I can beat Dr. Ninjario later. I quickly get ready for school. Then, I remember that today is show-and-tell. I put Webster, my tarantula, in his travel cage and pack him a crunchy cricket for lunch.

My best friends, Maddy and Jakey, get a sneak peek on the bus.

EMERGENCY DOOR

Show-and-tell is a blast! The whole class is mesmerized, and they ask so many questions. "What does Webster eat?" "Does he bite?" "Does he sleep?" "Does he poop?"

When I tell them I brought a cricket, they all beg to watch me feed it to Webster.

Later at recess, I run straight out to the soccer field. *Uh-oh*, Parker is playing. I'm a little scared of him.

We start the game, and Parker quickly scores three goals on Albert. "Haha! Three goals in three minutes!" he says. "You're the worst goalie ever!"

Albert cries and runs off the field.

A few minutes later, Maddy tries to stop the ball. It rolls right under her foot and goes straight into the goal. Parker yells at Maddy, "You're worse than Albert! Why don't you go join him in the cry baby corner?"

What Should DANNY Do?

Continue playing without responding? Go to page 72
Tell Parker to play nicely? Go to page 14

"What's wrong, Leo?" I ask.

"I forgot my lunch at home," he says. "My tummy hurts so much."

"I know how that feels," I say. "Last time I forgot my lunch at home, my super power tank emptied really fast."

I have an idea. I tell my friends, and they all agree.

We each give him a small part of our lunch, so we still have plenty left to eat.

"Wow." Leo says. "You guys are so nice."

Seeing how happy Leo is because of what we did reminds me that kindness is one of my most powerful superpowers. It's so easy to use, and it can make others so happy.

After lunch, it's time for science! Score! I love science! Last week we built volcanoes, and today we get to make them erupt with slimy lava! I'm so excited that I get started right away.

I mix the ingredients, but when I pour in the vinegar, nothing happens.

I try again. This time, I pour in half the bottle of vinegar, but still nothing happens.

All around the room, kids start cheering as their volcanoes erupt.

I try mixing everything again, and my slime feels perfectly gooey. I pour in the vinegar, but all I get is a stinky volcano that isn't erupting.

This is so frustrating, I feel like giving up and just playing with my slime.

What Should DANNY Do?

Keep trying to make his volcano erupt? Go to page 54
Give up and just play with his slime? Go to page 64

I don't raise my hand, and neither does anyone else. "OK," she says. "Please turn in your worksheets when you're done."

Uh-oh. This is confusing. I don't know where to start. Which numbers do I put on the line, and how? I try to use my super focus, but it isn't helping.

Just then, an idea pops into my head! I use my x-ray vision to look at Mario's paper.

"Please keep your eyes on your own paper," Ms. Blakely announces. Aw, man. How'd she know?

After a few minutes, the class starts turning in their worksheets. Ms. Blakely looks at my sheet and asks me why it's blank.

"I used invisible ink," I say.

Ms. Blakely doesn't laugh at my joke. "Danny, if you don't know how to do something, you should always ask," she says. "I'm going to write your parents a note and send some worksheets home with you so that you don't fall further behind."

When I get home, I show Mommy the note.

"Some of the world's smartest people ask the most questions," she says to me. "You should never be embarrassed that you're trying to learn something."

I turn on my super focus, and Mommy shows me how to use a number line. Now I have to do the worksheets. If I would have asked Ms. Blakely that question in class, I think it would have saved me a lot of time.

End
#6

I have the perfect idea. I turn my math worksheet over and draw a picture of MAD MADDY.

I show it to her but she starts crying and takes it straight to Ms. Blakely. *Uh-oh.*

"Who drew this?" she demands.

"Danny!" Maddy says, still crying.

"Danny, you'll need to stay in and see me after school," Ms. Blakely says.

Oh, no! Now I'm in serious trouble.

Later at lunch, Jakey and Maddy are mad at me, so I just sit alone.

After I finish eating, Mario crashes right into me. His chocolate pudding spills all over my shirt!

What Should DANNY Do?

Wash the pudding off? Go to page 68
Yell at Mario? Go to page 60

Superheroes don't give up that easily!

I start over, but this time I use my super focus to make sure my measurements are precise. Oh! It looks like I left out the baking soda last time! Maybe that's why it didn't work.

I pour in the vinegar, and--whoa!--my volcano has the gooiest, gloppiest eruption! The lava keeps oozing out!

WHOA!

Ms. Blakely comes over to me and says, "Danny, I saw that you had to remix your slime a few times. I'm proud of you for continuing to try hard even though things weren't going your way.

"Thanks, Ms. Blakely."

Jakey comes over to my table, and we play with each other's slime.

Later, Ms. Blakely calls for everyone's attention. The whole class quiets down.

"Someone in this class has made some excellent choices today. After recess, Maddy told me about how he helped convince someone to play nicely with everyone else. At lunch, I saw him gather food for someone who forgot their lunch at home."

Hmmm. Could she be talking about me?

Ms. Blakely continues, "Just now he worked extra hard on his science project and chose to not give up. This person definitely used their POWER TO CHOOSE wisely, so he deserves to be the P2C star of the week. Danny Miller, please come up to accept your award."

The entire class applauds.

Score! This is awesome!

Star of the Week

P2C

Awarded to

DANNY

When I get home, Mommy is so proud of me. She even lets me invite Jakey and Maddy over to test out my new zip line.

This must be how superheroes feel when they fly high above the city after a day of hard work.

End
#1

"Watch where you're going, meanie!" I yell.

Mario sneers. "At least I don't have mud all over my shirt."

I'm so mad, I throw the rest of my lunch at him. He throws his lunch back at me.

Mr. Kimbal

We get sent to the principal's office, and I have to go in first.

"Do you know why you're here, Danny?" Mr. Kimbal asks.

"I've had a terrible day," I say.

"Do you know why your day was so terrible?"

"I made a lot of poor choices."

I start to cry.

"I have to call your parents and ask them to pick you up," he says.

I cry even louder.

While I'm waiting for Mommy, Mr. Kimbal says "No matter what is happening to you, how you react is always a choice you make. If you use your POWER TO CHOOSE wisely tomorrow, I'm sure you'll have a much better day."

End #2

I hear more cheering as the final volcanoes erupt. No one is going to cheer for me and my dormant volcano. I crumple up the directions and throw them in the trash.

Just because my volcano isn't erupting doesn't mean I can't have fun. I pull the slime out and mix in more ingredients.

Eewww! This slime isn't turning out so well. I try to wipe it off my hands, but it gets all over the place.

Slime on my hands, slime on my shirt, slime in my hair! Yuck!

Later, Daddy comes home from work. "Cool volcano!" he says. "Did you make it erupt in class?"

"No," I say. "It was too hard."

"So, you couldn't get it to erupt *yet*," he says. "But how about we give it another try?"

I think about how hard it was at school, but if the other kids could do it, I know I can too.

"I'd like that," I say.

Daddy prints out the instructions, and I get straight to work. I turn on my super focus, and follow the instructions line by line.

It works! *Score!*

"Thanks for giving me another chance to use my POWER TO CHOOSE wisely, Daddy," I say.

"I'm so proud you did, Danny!"

End #4

Mario looks at my shirt. "Oops. Sorry about that," he says.

"It's OK, it was an accident," I say. "It looks like I fell in mud."

Mario and I laugh.

We go to the bathroom, and he helps me clean up.

After school, Ms. Blakely wants to talk to me about the picture I drew.

"Some days you might feel like everything is going wrong, but you can always change that by making better choices. Can you think of a time where you could have used your POWER TO CHOOSE wisely to improve your day?"

I think about how my recess could have been better if I would have played basketball, or how Maddy wouldn't be so upset with me if I would have apologized.

Now I know that using my POWER TO CHOOSE wisely is just as important at school as it is at home. I wish I'd figured that out a little sooner.

End #7

I think about how scared Maddy must have been.

"I'm really sorry about not taking better care of Webster, Maddy," I say when we walk out to lunch.

Maddy smiles. "I forgive you. I know you didn't do it on purpose."

I whisper, "Don't tell anyone, but I'm afraid of clowns."

She giggles and says, "Don't worry, I won't tell."

When I get home, I tell Mommy about how Webster got loose and how recess was super boring.

"It's a good thing you chose to apologize to Maddy," she says. "Your day could have been much worse."

I think about everything that happened and how it may have been different if I made better choices. I think tomorrow will be a better day if I use my POWER TO CHOOSE wisely.

End #8

Maddy runs to the bathroom crying.

After a minute, Parker is guarding me. I get so scared that I freeze. He steals the ball, then scores a goal.

"Ha! Danny, you must be the worst player in the whole school," he says. "You should stay off the field forever."

Tears come to my eyes. I run away to hide before Parker can see.

I'm embarrassed for letting him push me around. I don't feel like such a superhero.

I stay in my hiding spot until recess is over.

39

Go to page 12

Danny

Meet (the real) Danny, the authors' adorable nephew, who served as inspiration for the main character. He's a real superhero in training, full of energy, and never misbehaves.😉

Danny's First Adventure

Check out the #1 Amazon Best Seller, *What Should Danny Do?* in which Danny uses his POWER TO CHOOSE at home!

About the Authors

Ganit, a former teacher, and Adir, an astrophysics junkie, are parents to four amazing kids. When they're not busy teaching them about their POWER TO CHOOSE, they enjoy writing, painting, and date nights at Target.

About the Illustrator

Mat Sadler is an Illustrator of things. He lives with his wife and two kids in England (but he doesn't sound like Hugh Grant—or Pierce Brosnan for that matter. He's from Essex).

Emma

Ms Blakely

Maddy

Albert

Danny

Alexis

Danny

Maddy

Jakey

Bruce

Dear Parents & Educators,

Children enjoy the book best, and learn the most, when reading through multiple versions of the story. Because this may be your child's first exposure to a story in this format, you may need to encourage them to make different choices "just to see what happens."

Through repetition and discussion, your child will be empowered with the understanding that their choices will shape their days, and ultimately their lives, into what they will be.

Ganit & Adir

What Should Danny Do? School Day / by Ganit & Adir Levy.

Summary: Danny, a superhero in training, learns the importance of making good choices at school.
Levy, Ganit & Adir, authors
Sadler, Mat, illustrator
Klempner, Rebecca, editor
ISBN 9780692914373
Visit www.whatshoulddannydo.com
Printed in the United States of America
Reinforced binding
First Edition, November 2018
10 9 8 7 6 5 4 3 2 1

Sarah

Zoe